# THIS BOOK BELONGS TO:

**SECRET IDENTITY**

Do not fill this bit in or
Dr Septic will know who you are
...............................................................

**SUPERHERO NAME**

...............................................................

## OTHER BOOKS BY MICHAEL COX

Johnny Catbiscuit to the Rescue!

Johnny Catbiscuit and the Abominable Snotmen!

Johnny Catbiscuit and the Stolen Secrets!

Little Fred Riding Hood

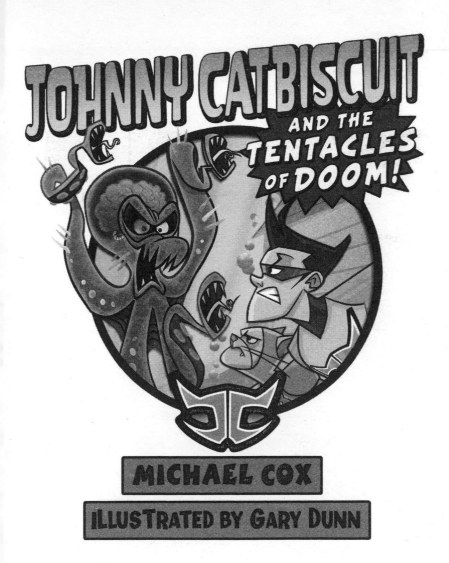

# JOHNNY CATBISCUIT AND THE TENTACLES OF DOOM!

## MICHAEL COX

### ILLUSTRATED BY GARY DUNN

EGMONT

*To Ted and Joyce Cox*

# EGMONT
*We bring stories to life*

*Johnny Catbiscuit and the Tentacles of Doom!*
First published in Great Britain 2008
by Egmont UK Limited
239 Kensington High Street
London W8 6SA

ISBN 978 1 4052 3738 3

1 3 5 7 9 10 8 6 4 2

A CIP catalogue record for this title is available from the British Library

Printed and bound in Great Britain by the CPI Group

# CONTENTS

## CHAPTER ONE
# THE LITTLE FISH

'Please can I have a bunch of bananas for my gran?' said twelve-year-old Wayne Bunn.

'Why?' laughed Mr Marsden. 'Have you grown tired of her?'

'I beg your pardon?' said Wayne, looking slightly taken aback.

'I'm joking, Wayne!' chuckled the greengrocer. 'You sounded like you wanted to do a swap! You know, a bunch of bananas . . . for your gran!'

'Oh, I get you!' laughed Wayne. 'Sorry, Mr Marsden. I was thinking about the dried-up rivers.'

'Oh, that!' shrugged Mr Marsden. 'I'm sure there's a perfectly simple explanation. Such as this dry weather we're having?'

'Or farmers pumping out the water to irrigate their fields?' added Mrs Marsden. 'I wouldn't give it a second thought, young Wayne! Boys of your age have got far better things to be doing than worrying about rivers!'

However, despite such words of reassurance, Wayne just knew that something odd was going on. The mighty Trout had slowed to a muddy trickle. The normally deep and tranquil

H₂Oooze had been reduced to just a few pathetic puddles. And the roaring Torrent was no more than a dribble.

Wayne left the greengrocers and went to the bank of the river Torrent. He stared at the dried-up watercourse, trying to make sense of the mystery of the vanishing rivers. Only a short while ago, the scene before him had been so different. The sparkling Torrent had been alive with shoals of speckled trout, scores of shimmering sticklebacks, multitudes of minnows, wildly wriggling eels, darting kingfishers, high-stepping heron . . . and much, much more! And now they were all gone, seeking shelter

3

and survival in the few brackish ponds and puddles that were left. There was no river life.

Or was there? All at once, Wayne spotted a flash of silver in one of the rocky puddles. Dropping to his knees, he instantly recognised it as a lone flipper-fish, flapping and twitching among the stones and boulders where the Torrent's crystal-clear waters had raced and gurgled just a few weeks ago. Putting down his shopping, he carefully scooped up the tiny fish and gently cupped it in his hands, intending to rush it to the nearest pond. But, before he could act, the pitiful creature gazed up at him, opened its tiny mouth, and spoke.

4

'Forget it, Wayne Bunn!' it gasped, as Wayne cradled it in his palms. 'I'm a goner!'

Then it paused and added, 'Or should I say, "Forget it, **JOHNNY CATBISCUIT!**"'

Wayne gave a start. 'So you know who I am?' he asked.

'Of course I do!' said the fish. 'As do all the animals. And we also know of the many brave

deeds which you and your sidekick, Felix Pawson, have carried out in your heroic defence of creatures great and small. Your fame has spread far beyond the Realms of Normality. And you mustn't worry, your secret identities are safe with us. We are all eternally grateful for your never-ending kindness and concern for our safety and well-being.'

'So please let me try and save you!' whispered Wayne, who, like his other 'super' self, the amazing Johnny Catbiscuit, was fluent in dozens of animal languages, including Ferret, Field Mouse, Flounder, Flipper-Fish and Fruit Bat.

'No, don't!' gasped the fish, as Wayne

carefully laid it in a puddle. 'I'm beyond all help. And time is short. You have only a few hours left. Possibly even less! Please listen to what I have to tell you!'

'All right!' said Wayne, suddenly aware that disaster loomed. 'What is it, little fish?'

'I have a message for you!' gasped the fish. 'I've come from the high mountains where all the great rivers begin. The big fish – the double bass, the monstrous pike, the electrostatic eel and the silver-spotted salmon – sent me. I was the only one small enough to make the journey. But it was full of danger, taking longer than I expected. I may already be too late!'

'But what is your message?' said Wayne.

'Many bad things are being done a long way away from here,' said the fish. 'And, for your beautiful homelands, the Realms of Normality, the . . . cons . . . cons?'

'Consequences?' said Wayne.

'Yes, that's it! Conquessences!' wheezed the little fish.

'Actually, it's consequences,' said Wayne.

'Yes, of course!' said the fish. 'I'm sorry.' It paused. Then, mustering what little strength it had left, it went on. 'Yes, the conquessences for the land, animals and people you love so dearly and protect so courageously are going to be

terrible! That is why I have been sent to seek you out. For you and Felix Pawson are the only ones who can save them! Unless you act immediately, thousands will perish most horribly! You must save them, Johnny Catbiscuit! Listen carefully, this is what you must do. First, you have to –'

But then the exhausted fish halted, its tiny mouth opening and closing frantically as it struggled to continue. Wayne held his breath. The little creature was obviously near its end.

'Go on, little fellow!' he urged, desperate to hear what the fish had to say. 'Tell me what I must do!'

'Johnny Catbiscuit . . . you . . . must . . . you . . . must . . .' gasped the fish. But it was no good. It couldn't go on. It was utterly worn out from flipping and flopping its way from puddle to puddle in its desperate quest to bring Wayne its all-important message. The message he would now never hear. For, as he watched with a sinking heart, it twitched a couple of times, flapped its fins, then went very, very still.

'Gone!' muttered Wayne. 'And I never even knew your name.'

The fish opened one eye.

'It's Gill!' it said. 'My name is Gill.'

And then it did die.

Wayne laid the little body on the grass and began to scoop out a tiny grave in the damp earth of the river bed. As he did, his mind whirled, urgently sifting and sorting through all of the possible implications of the little creature's unspoken message. And, inevitably, his every thought led him to the same awful conclusion. The fish's heroic journey from the high mountains could only mean one thing.

That most hated, ruthless and feared individual on all of Space-Speck Earth, Dr Septacemius J. Septic, was about to embark on yet another of his fiendish plans to enslave the good folk and innocent creatures of the Realms of Normality. Just as he had been trying to do ever since Wayne was knee high to a terrapin.

But, thank goodness, so far, all of Dr Septic's sinister schemes had come to nought, all thanks to the heroic efforts of the Superheroes of the Realms of Normality. And, more recently, all thanks to the outstandingly heroic efforts of those two most remarkable of all superheroes, Johnny Catbiscuit and Felix Pawson!

Wayne raced through the streets of Nicetown as fast as his skinny legs would carry him, desperate to reach his gran's, the place where he'd lived since becoming an orphan. For there, in the very ordinary-looking black bin liner which lay hidden behind his wardrobe, was the super-outfit which would transform him from scrawny schoolboy Wayne Bunn to supremely successful superhero and saviour of all that is good and decent – Johnny Catbiscuit. And alongside that super-outfit lay an identical, but smaller one. That of his sidekick and best friend Felix Pawson, the courageous and cool cat who had been his constant companion

13

since the day Johnny had rescued him from the secret experimental laboratories of Dr Septic's evil partner, St Bernard Muttshoes, along with his own pets and hundreds of other innocent creatures.* The same Felix Pawson whose n'er-do-well twin brother Roland, to Felix's enduring shame and regret, was the lap-cat of the loathsome Dr Septic.

After reaching his gran's house and finding her asleep in her armchair, Wayne paused to briefly scribble her a note, and to greet his animal pals: Mr Parks, his pet spaniel, Miss Purrfect, his kitten and Warren, his rabbit. Then, bounding up the stairs two at a time,

* Please see *Johnny Catbiscuit to the Rescue!*

he began to focus on the coming conflict. He knew, as ever, that it would test him and Felix to their limits – as had all their previous encounters with Dr Septic. Nevertheless, as well as these feelings of apprehension, Wayne had a positively dizzying surge of excitement coursing through his veins! For he knew that in the next few minutes he would be experiencing that thrill to end all thrills! He would be turning into the all-powerful superhero . . . *JOHNNY CATBISCUIT!*

## CHAPTER TWO
# SEPTIC TOWERS

At the same moment, hundreds of miles away
from cosy Nicetown, among wind-blasted crags
and raven-flecked cliffs, someone else was also
tingling with excitement. High in his mist-
shrouded mountain fortress, Septic Towers, Dr
Septacemius J. Septic was pacing the seal-skin
carpet of his inner sanctum, muttering insanely.
He was looking forward to what he hoped
would be the almost-certain annihilation of

the young superhero who, along with his accursed cat, had brought him nothing but disappointment, frustration and failure.

From the left sleeve of the evil genius's moleskin dressing gown there poked a glittering artificial hand, clutching something small and soft. At first glance, the little object might have been mistaken for a fluffy toy. But on closer examination it was plain to see that it was nothing of the kind. It was a lifelike model of Felix Pawson, perfect in every detail, down to its real cat's fur and tiny claws. In his other, 'natural' hand, Dr Septic gripped a second tiny mannequin. This one was sheathed in silver

17

and clad in a tiny golden cape bearing the initials 'JC'. It was an equally realistic and brilliantly detailed likeness of Johnny Catbiscuit.

On the opposite side of the room from Dr Septic was an enormous fish tank. In it, there writhed a squirming shoal of purplish-pink, jelly-like creatures, all of them so hideous and grotesque that just one glimpse of their loathsome features would have given even the toughest person nightmares for years to come. Some had huge bulging, hooded eyes and beaks like birds of prey. Others had three, or even four, huge lidless eyes and mouths like leeches, filled with needle-sharp teeth. Others had no

eyes at all. And others, covered all over with pulsating pink pustules, had eyes on stalks and fat, warty snouts.

But what all of them had . . . was tentacles! Dozens and dozens of frantically waving tentacles. Like a great forest of flickering, fearsome fingers. There were short stumpy ones, ridged like armour. Branched ones, with other, smaller tentacles coming off them. Ones with fanged mouths at their ends. Ones which ended in

huge clawed 'hands'! Spiral ones. Rainbow-coloured ones. Ones so long and thin they looked like giant worms, strands of spaghetti or lengths of hair. Some stretched three metres away from their owners!

Dr Septic went over to the tank. With a sigh of satisfaction, he dropped the tiny cat model

into the water. Hardly had it hit the surface than the hideous purple creatures began to tear and pull at it, quickly reducing it to a mess of soggy fur and mangled limbs. Next, Dr Septic grasped the figure of Johnny in both hands, twisting it savagely and pulling off the head. Then, shrieking with insane laughter, he hurled the body into the tank and roared with delight as the horrid creatures turned their attention to this. He prepared to do the same with the severed head. However, at that moment, there was a knock at the door.

Dr Septic slipped the 'head' of Johnny Catbiscuit into his pocket, then in a voice

22

sounding like rusty axe heads and machete blades being tumbled in a concrete mixer, he barked, 'Come in, Professor Troll!'

The door opened to reveal a plump, red-faced man wearing a pale green surgeon's tunic, bloodstained butcher's apron, baggy pink shorts and crimson bow tie. His brow glistened with perspiration and his slug-like lips quivered with excitement, almost as if he expected to be fed a tasty titbit at any moment. In one hand, he held a detonator of the sort used to blast tons of rock from the sides of quarries. In the other, he held an enormous, half-eaten peanut butter sandwich, which he squeezed constantly,

23

causing great globbets of its contents to fall on to Dr Septic's study carpet. Professor Elvis Troll was Dr Septic's closest ally and 'fixer' of all things wicked. A man whose ability to turn dreams into nightmares was without equal.

'Well, Professor?' hissed the scarecrow-like Dr Septic, towering at least a metre above his podgy little assistant. 'Is everything ready?'

'It is, your Perfectness,' replied the Professor, bowing so low that his button-nose almost touched the tip of Dr Septic's rhinoceros-hide, hobnail riding boots. 'Last night's storms could not have come at a better time. The aqua-gauges have finally reached the eighty-metre mark.'

24

'Perfect, my dear Elvis!' crooned Dr Septic, patting his little accomplice's bald and shiny head. 'And what about the . . .' He trailed off, simply nodding towards the nightmarish fish tank.

'Oh, they are more than ready!' grinned Professor Troll. 'In fact, if you would care to follow me, your Magnificentness, you will now be able to feast your eyes upon the FOUL and FRIGHTFUL fruits of my labours! But I must warn you, they are not a pretty sight!'

Dr Septic cackled evilly and hissed, 'Excellent . . . I can hardly wait!'

## CHAPTER THREE
# TROUBLE'S COMING!

'Wake up, FP!' yelled Wayne, causing his best pal to leap a metre into the air. 'Trouble's coming!'

Felix Pawson landed back on the bed where he'd been snoozing peacefully after a night out with Fu-Fu, his Siamese girlfriend. 'Where's the trouble, superboy?' he said, instantly alert.

Wayne was already pulling Johnny Catbiscuit's super-outfit from the black bin liner. First out was his silver vest with the initials 'JC'. Next

came a glittering golden cape, golden gloves and a pair of winged boots. Then his silver mask. And finally, his biometric, plasma-chuffed wrist-pod. He had it all on in a flash. Then he took a deep breath, and said:

'*The Realms are under threat*
*From what, I know not yet*
*But however they're beset*
*I'm prepared to wager*
*Dr Septic's behind the danger!*'

As he spoke, an astonishing transformation overcame him. First, he was enveloped in a bluish-green glow which sparked and danced about him, occasionally turning to shades of

27

orange and yellow. Then, as this unearthly light faded, his body began to change. He grew taller, his shoulders and chest became broader, like those of a world-class gymnast. Then his stick-like legs and arms changed from puny into hugely muscled limbs a champion bodybuilder would have envied. And finally, his face changed: his jaw became stronger and firmer, his skin took on a deep and healthy tan, his eyes sparkled with confidence. He now had the stunning good looks of a heart-throb film star.

His transformation was complete. Gone were Wayne Bunn's skinny shoulders. Gone too were his bony chest and sticky-out ears. No

longer did he look like you could have knocked him down with your little finger. Now it would have taken a runaway truck. And even that would have come off worse.

Now it was time for Felix to undergo *his* transformation. First, he grew to twice his normal size, his muscles becoming sinewy and beautifully defined. Soon he was the size of a lynx, rather than a domestic cat. Next, his legs grew and, as they did, he rose up on his rear limbs, standing a metre tall. And finally, his front paws changed into a pair of nimble-looking hands, complete with thumbs and fingers, but still keeping their lethal-looking claws.

Felix reached into the black bin liner, pulled out a similarly spectacular, but smaller, costume, and put it on with equal speed. Then, with a devil-may-care grin, he said, 'OK, partner, ready to roll!' And he leapt on to Johnny Catbiscuit's broad shoulders, spread his forelegs wide and firmly grasped Johnny's super-tunic in his powerful new hands.

But before the dynamic duo flew off, there was something Johnny had to do. Flipping open his wrist-pod, he tapped in *W-0000-5H*, pressed the hash key and chose *OPTION 6*.

A girl's smiling face instantly appeared on the 3D screen. She was wearing a smart green

cap with an '**SSSS**' badge on it.

'Hi, Johnny!' she said. 'Thank you for calling Superhero Support Service Solutions. How may I help you?'

'Hi, Jatinder!' said Johnny. 'I'll make this brief. Dr Septic's about to pull something big. But I've no idea what! All I can tell you is that

it's got something to do with the dried-up rivers. So we're heading north to do some sticky-beaking! In the meantime, please alert **CAPTAIN UNSTOPPABLE**, *BODACIOUS BABE*, **Susan the Human-Post-It-Note**, *THE SILVER RIPPLE* and all the other superheroes to an imminent threat: level crimson with a hint of magenta. The moment I know more, I'll be in touch. Now, I must fly!'

'Will do, Johnny! Good luck with the sticky-beaking! And take care!' replied the ever-helpful Jatinder. 'Thank you for calling Superhero Support Service Solutions.'

Hardly had these words left her mouth than

32

Johnny threw open his bedroom window, took a deep breath, then shot skywards, on course for those distant mountains. He felt certain it was here, he and Felix would find the answer to the mystery of the vanishing rivers, and would also be able to fulfill that little fish's dying wish. *Whatever* it took!

Dear Gran
Have popped out with Felix
for some fresh air.
Might be gone for some time.
Love Wayne XX
PS: Have left shopping on kitchen table.

## CHAPTER FOUR
## a mere 'Hobby'

Dr Septic followed Professor Troll out of his study to a dizzyingly high glass observatory. It was perched at the top of the tallest tower and bristled with monitor screens, control panels and surveillance devices. And some very lethal-looking weaponry! From here, it was possible to see for miles. On a clear day, peering through the laser-enhanced viewfinder of his gigantic

spectrographic telescope, Dr Septic was able to observe the comings and goings of the towns, villages and cities of the Realms of Normality. Only that morning, he'd been watching an extremely scrawny schoolboy crouching on the bank of the dried-up river Torrent, apparently engaged in some sort of nature study. Though what the boy was studying, Dr Septic could not

35

tell. Even his hyper-powerful telescope couldn't pick up that sort of detail! And what he also didn't know (thank goodness!) was the secret identity of that boy.

But now Dr Septic looked down on the vast central courtyard of Septic Towers. And as he did so, he gave a cry of pleasure, clapping his hands in delight (not an easy thing to do when one of them is made from pure titanium).

Below him, in a huge pool, swam dozens of hideous, tentacled aquatic creatures like those horrors in the fish tank in his study. But not only were these bizarre creations a hundred times *more* terrifying in their hideousness,

they were also **ENORMOUS!**

Only a mind as warped and brilliant as Professor Troll's could have dreamed up and created such hideous creatures. And only a mind as evil, ruthless and power-crazed as Dr Septic's could have asked him to do so.

'Magnificent, my dear Troll!' croaked Dr Septic. 'You have done us proud! Your personal talent for bringing to life the terrors which inhabit your sad little mind are unsurpassed!'

'Oh you flatter me, your Greatness,' said the Professor. 'It is a mere hobby! A mere hobby!'

Then he gave a conceited smirk and added, 'I think my little "treasures" down there will

37

keep the superheroes extremely busy!'

'Oh, yessss!' purred Dr Septic. 'They won't be able to save their own skins! Or the citizens and creatures of the Realms of Normality.'

He absent-mindedly rolled the little head of Johnny Catbiscuit around his palm, jabbing it viciously with his lethal, false fingers.

At this, a look of anxiety clouded Professor Troll's moist, pink features. 'And the one they call Catbiscuit?' he mumbled. 'Do you think he will present a problem?'

'Oh no!' whispered Dr Septic. 'Special *arrangements* have been made for him! Johnny Catbiscuit will give us no trouble! Nor

will his little sidekick!'
He dropped the head
on the floor and began
to grind it to a pulp
with the heel of his hobnail riding boot.

Professor Troll let out a huge sigh of relief and beamed with pleasure. 'So what are we waiting for, your Loveliness!' he cried, waving the detonator in Dr Septic's face. 'I have one hundred of these little beauties installed in the dam walls, along with several thousand tons of TNT, dynamite and gelignite. Not to mention some really ace fireworks, left over from last year's Bonfire Night. All we have to do is press

the plunger! Then . . . BOOOOM!'

'Yes, BOOOOOM! BOOOOOM! BOOOOOOOM!' roared Dr Septic, raising his arms high in the air and dancing wildly around the room, his ice-grey eyes glinting madly and his razor-slim lips drawn back to reveal his chipped and moss-dappled tombstone teeth.

'But of course, first we must release our little "treasures"!' yelled Professor Troll, taking a huge bite from his sandwich and showering Dr Septic with blobs of peanut butter.

'And there is no time like the present!' screamed Dr Septic, seizing what was left of the

40

sandwich and stuffing it in his own mouth, then chewing it with such ferocity that Professor Troll feared he would next take a bite out of *him*.

But, to Professor Troll's huge relief, he didn't. He simply leapt at the large red lever on the control panel before them, grasped it with both hands, and gave it a mighty yank!

Nothing happened at first. Then, after several tension-filled seconds, there came a great swooshing sound from the pool below them, as sections of its huge floor smoothly slid apart. An instant later, the aquatic horrors in the pool were spinning wildly out of control in the great whirlpool caused by thousands of gallons of

water suddenly being sucked into the massive chasm. The water **ROILED** and **SWIRLED** and **CHURNED** in a thrashing, bubbling frenzy of sound and movement, as if an enormous plug had just been pulled from a giant's bathtub. The massive creatures did their best to resist its pull; they writhed and thrashed, their giant jaws and scaly beaks snapping wildly, their vast blubbery bodies wriggling and flopping, their serpentine tentacles snaking this way and that.

But they could not resist the force of gravity. After a few minutes of chaos, confusion and commotion, there was an almighty gurgling sound and, a moment later, the last of the

42

water gave a great surge, then disappeared down the giant hole. Suddenly, apart from the pitiful screechings and thrashings of one wretched beast, which had, quite gruesomely, become trapped between two of the sliding floor plates, the pool was silent and empty.

But were the evil genius and his horrid

henchman dismayed? Of course they weren't! Apart from that single casualty, all had gone according to plan. They rubbed their hands with glee, knowing that the monsters had tumbled into the great underground river which flowed beneath Dr Septic's mountain fortress, and would be swept along by its swift current. Then, eventually bursting into bright daylight at the entrance to the great ravine known as the Gorges of Hell, they would be carried through a series of bends, over tumbling, sheer-sided cataracts and finally into a vast artificial lake. This had been created by Dr Septic's engineers just a few weeks earlier, when they

had dammed the upper reaches of the Torrent, the H₂Oooze and the Trout. There, the monsters would be held before being unleashed on the Realms of Normality.

'You have excelled yourself, Professor!' cried Dr Septic, clapping Professor Troll on the shoulder. 'And now it is time for me to leave! For I must make all haste to the Realms of Normality, where I have some extremely pressing unfinished business to conclude!' And so saying, he gave Professor Troll a most evil and conspiratorial wink.

'And, Professor Troll!' Dr Septic added menacingly. 'I am leaving my dearest and

45

cruellest in your most capable care. Ensure no harm befalls her. Or you will have me to answer to! The next time we three meet will be in Nothingham-on-Torrent, hopefully amidst scenes of doom, despair, danger, devastation, damage, disbelief, disaster, dismay, destruction, dis–' But then Dr Septic ran out of scary words beginning with 'd', so he quickly left.

As Dr Septic raced off to conclude his unfinished business, Professor Troll and Dr Septic's dearest and cruellest, the horrendous Janice Evil, would make their way to the rocky bluff which overlooked the vast lake. Then, as soon as they were satisfied that the waters

were **SEETHING** with the Professor's horrible creations, and the moment they received the go-ahead from their evil master, the awful Janice would press a plunger, setting off a series of massive **EXPLOSIONS**. And the walls of those three huge dams would give way in a great **ERUPTION** of fire and rock and ear-splitting sound.

Then all those countless billions of litres of water would go rushing down the Torrent Valley, carrying their cargo of terror to the unsuspecting villages, towns and cities of the Realms of Normality.

## CHAPTER FIVE
# SUPERSONIC JOHNNY

As Johnny Catbiscuit and Felix Pawson soared northwards, following the course of Torrent Valley to those distant peaks and uplands where horrors and challenges awaited them, Johnny was only too aware of the fish's desperate words: 'I may already be too late!'

Remembering that grim warning, and with a yell of, '**HOLD ON TO YOUR WHISKERS, FP!**', he flew faster than he'd ever flown before! So

fast that both Johnny and Felix's faces became flattened and distorted, like the faces of people descending the steepest and fastest stretches of a roller-coaster ride. So fast that they actually overtook a supersonic airliner as it flew a party of school children home. This awesome spectacle gave the kids such a shock that they grabbed their cameras – otherwise no one would have believed they'd seen the legendary duo rocketing past them. Johnny obligingly gave them all a cheery wave and a cry of, '**YOO HOO!**'

Felix simply gave them an extremely cheesy grin, and a playful yell of, '**EAT OUR VAPOUR TRAIL, JUNIOR GLOBE-TROTTERS!**', because if

he had relaxed his grip on Johnny's shoulders for a moment, he would have hurtled off into the stratosphere! None of them knew it then, but this wasn't the only time their paths would cross on that amazing day.

The supersonic pair were soon within twenty minutes' flying-time of the mountains. This delighted Johnny so much he hoped that they could still stop the unknown, but imminent, disaster his arch-enemy was about to unleash.

But then, just after the plucky pals had passed over Nothingham-on-Torrent, with its cobbled streets and leafy squares, an urgent bleeping came from Johnny's plasma-chuffed

51

wrist-pod. Without any decrease in speed, he flipped the device to 'Talk' mode.

It was Jatinder from **SSSS**. And, from the look on her face, it was obviously bad news.

'Johnny!' she said. 'We need your help. And fast! We've just had a call. Safe Pastures is on fire. And if someone doesn't get there soon, hundreds will be burned alive!'

**'SHIVERING SHOELACES!'** Johnny was aghast. Safe Pastures was the remote Northern Realms regional HQ of the St Rolfus of Ozissi Poorly Animal Sanctuary. He and Felix brought the sick or wounded creatures they'd plucked from the jaws of disaster to Safe Pastures. And it was

there that they had seen these creatures begin
the long road to recovery, as they grazed the
lush meadows, or snuggled down in the warm
stables, hutches and kennels, knowing that
they were in safe hands.

'You must put your mission on hold!' said
Jatinder. 'Lives are in peril!'

But Johnny and Felix didn't need to be told

that. Their super-duties and responsibilities lay in the here-and-now. And the here-and-now was those endangered animals.

So Johnny and Felix wheeled to the west, setting course for Safe Pastures.

Six minutes later, they saw the smoke, huge clouds of it billowing up from the sanctuary's hospital block and feed store. And then they spotted the panic-stricken animals, milling around in confusion, neighing, barking, howling and screeching with terror.

'**CRAWLING KUMQUATS!**' Felix shuddered at the sight below.

Swiftly descending to a point just a hundred

metres above the blaze, the choking black smoke now filling their lungs and stinging their eyes, the pals spied a group of people wearing the familiar carers' uniforms of the Order of St Rolfus. All of them were waving their arms and desperately pointing towards a spot which was, as yet, unaffected by the fire. It had been Johnny's intention to swoop down to the water tank, then empty its contents on to the heart of the blaze. But those good folk were beckoning and pointing so frantically, he assumed they must know something that he didn't. So he landed at the spot they indicated.

Exactly as Dr Septic had planned.

## CHAPTER SIX
# a RIGHT MeSH

Suddenly, there were four ear-splitting cracks. A second later, Johnny Catbiscuit and Felix Pawson were entangled in the folds of a huge net. A net launched by four small rockets and woven from super-strong, triple-braided **THEWLON**™. It was so tough that even Johnny was unable to tear it apart. Though to be fair, at that moment, he was also being beaten by the 'vets' and 'carers'. As was Felix! Horrid clubs

56

had appeared in the normally kind and gentle hands of those devotees of St Rolfus!

'**CRUMBLING CODFISH!**' yelled Felix, as he reeled under a welter of blows. '**WHAT THE HELTER-SKELTER IS HAPPENING?**'

But Johnny wasn't listening. He was staring at the scarecrow-like 'chief vet', who stood away from the melee, cackling like a lunatic.

The 'chief vet' who he recognised as Dr Septic!

Two minutes later Dr Septic's thugs had extinguished the 'inferno' and several rapid-fire harpoon launchers were trained on Johnny and Felix. Although this probably wasn't necessary, as the pals were now so thoroughly trapped in

the **THEWLON**$^{TM}$ **NETTING** that they looked like a pair of Ancient Egyptian mummies!

'Remarkable what impression you can create with a few burning tyres, isn't it, Mr Catsick?' hissed Dr Septic, in a voice which reminded the duo of a basket full of spitting cobras.

'DR SEPTIC, YOU SCUM-SUCKING SLEAZEBALL!' muttered Johnny, furious with himself for having been duped. 'How low can you go? Terrifying the lives out of these innocent creatures so that you could lure us into a trap!'

'Oh, I don't know! They'll get over it!' smirked Dr Septic, nodding towards the real staff of the Sanctuary, who were in the feed

store, stripped of their uniforms and bound and gagged. Their panic-stricken eyes sent frantic messages of apology and regret to the superhero they admired most on Space-Speck Earth.

'I don't mean them!' muttered Johnny. 'I mean all those poor animals.'

'I do realise that!' snarled Dr Septic. 'But, Mr Gingerbiscuit . . . you ain't seen nothing yet!'

He pointed to a group of his hench-thugs, who were building an enormous bonfire by the entrance to the feed store and splashing it with high octane aviation fuel. There were two wooden stakes in its centre. Other thugs were rounding up the animals, prodding and kicking them as they herded them into the feed store.

'You wouldn't?' gasped Felix, as Dr Septic's despicable intentions became horribly clear.

'Of course I would!' smiled Dr Septic. 'This time it's going to be the real thing! The first fire was simply to get you here. You see, I had to

meet you one last time, Mr Catnip! I knew you wouldn't be able to ignore all these creatures in great peril. My call to the authorities was passed on to **SSSS** immediately. Just as I knew it would be! And now, Mr Catkin –'

But he was interrupted by the wail of sirens and the screech of tyres.

'Ah, the fire brigade are here!' said Dr Septic. 'Otto, please go and tell them that we have everything under control. All thanks to the prompt arrival of a certain young superhero!'

One of Dr Septic's thugs, dressed in the outfit of a senior vet, obediently sprinted down the drive. A few moments later there was a shout

of, 'All right, mate! Glad you got it sorted! We had a feeling Johnny Catbiscuit would beat us to it! Where *would* we be without him?'

A moment later, the fire engines were on their way back to Nothingham-on-Torrent.

By the time Otto returned, Johnny and Felix were securely bound to the stakes at the centre of the huge bonfire.

Dr Septic took a box of matches from his pocket and grinned his evil grin.

'**YOU MONSTER!**' hissed Felix.

'At least spare the animals and staff!' cried Johnny. 'They've done you no harm!'

'I can't!' hissed Dr Septic. 'I want you and

62

63

your sidekick to go out in a blaze of er, infamy, Mr Catlitter! Rather than a blaze of glory! And what could be a better end for the saviour of all creatures than to fail so many of them at their hour of need? The names Johnny Catbiscuit and Felix Pawson will be in the "Superhero Hall of Shame". To be reviled for ever!'

Now Dr Septic turned to the horrible Otto, saying, 'A couple of metres of fuse will be enough. We don't want it going up too soon, or those firefighters will be back!'

Then, as Otto lay the fuse to ignite the bonfire, Dr Septic tapped a key on his talk-pod. 'Professor Troll,' he oozed. 'You will be pleased

to know that the "mice" are in the "trap"!
Please tell my nearest and cruellest to do that
"thing"! I will join you both shortly.'

Dr Septic had just returned his talk-pod to his
pocket when there was an ENORMOUS EXPLOSION
to the north of them. So enormous that it rattled
windows and shook the earth. It was followed
by a second, even louder bang. Then a third.
And as the sound of those ominous eruptions
rumbled and echoed around those far-off peaks
and valleys, Dr Septic lit the fuse.

Three minutes later, a convoy of ten all-terrain
vehicles, each one carrying ten heavily-armed
thugs, and with inflatable motor dinghies

strapped to their roofs, roared out of Safe Pastures. They were followed by Dr Septic in his enormous all-chrome, massively be-finned and be-bumpered limousine. And as they raced away from the sanctuary, a flicker of flame raced *towards* the fuel-drenched bonfire surrounding Johnny and Felix.

No matter how much they struggled, they were held firm, like flies in a web. Such was the tightness of the netting and the thickness of its layers that even Johnny's super-strength was no match for it.

'Well, Johnny Catbiscuit,' said Felix. 'This is another fine old mesh you've got us into!'

## CHAPTER SEVEN
# BOOM!

When Janice Evil pressed that plunger, setting off those three **GIGANTIC** explosions, the effect was astonishing. Both on her and the dam wall! Suddenly, the air was filled with flames, acrid black smoke, flying rock and the deafening roar of all those billions and billions of litres of water cascading into the valley below.

'Oh, look at the lovely water feature! And all

the pretty fireworks!' squealed Janice, who, though Dr Septic was reluctant to admit it, was three times as barmy as him. Then she added, 'You can come out now, Professor Troll!'

For Janice, rather than taking cover, had stood at the edge of the dam which had held back the great lake, while Professor Troll cowered in a concrete bunker. And she hadn't fared too badly! OK, she was drenched from head-to-toe, her face was blacker than her black mamba-skin dungarees, her normally straight hair was standing on-end in a startling zigzag style, and her eyebrows had disappeared. But, apart from that, she was fine. She was

jumping up and down, pointing and squealing with excitement, as Professor Troll's aquatic monsters poured through the hole in the dam wall.

'Oooh, I say!' she said shrilly. 'You have been busy! And aren't they, er . . . unusual!'

This was something of an understatement.

Passing though the wall as she spoke was a sort of octopus, well more of a 'polypus', in that it had at least fifteen massive tentacles. It was the size of a small hovercraft and its enormous, pulpy and gelatinous-looking body was covered with big warty nodules. Each nodule had a set of bright crimson 'cupid' lips. Projecting from its face were three huge, bulbous eyes, which swivelled about, hungrily seeking out a victim. And below them was a lethal-looking beak, like that of a monstrous parakeet. But what was *really* remarkable about this terrifying monstrosity was its see-through flesh. Every twist and turn of its innards were completely visible! As was

70

its lunch, which appeared to be half a dozen smaller versions of itself. Obviously the runts of Professor Troll's loathsome litter.

Yet more of the dam wall fell away and the huge breach suddenly became filled with such a rush and tangle of monstrosities that all Janice saw were tentacles, tentacles and more tentacles! And all of them breathtaking in their diversity. This really was tentacle heaven! Or tentacle hell! It depended on your point of view.

But Janice was well impressed! '**SOOOPER! SOOOPER! SOOOPER! SOOOOPER!**' she shrieked, tickling Professor Troll under his many chins. 'You are a clever little robot, aren't you!'

'I'm not a robot!' muttered the outraged Professor Troll. 'I'm a *professor*!'

'Oh no, I think you'll find you're very much mistaken!' said Janice. 'Because Septikins told me you were. And Septikins knows everything! So there! You really *are* a little robot!'

But Professor Troll was no longer taking any notice of the bonkers Janice. Because if he had, he may have said something to upset her. And that would have landed him in hot water with Dr Septic. Quite literally! It wasn't just lobsters which were boiled alive at Septic Towers!

Instead, Professor Troll was doing a calculation. He'd just worked out that his wall of water a

his little 'treasures' would be sweeping into
Nothingham-on-Torrent in only thirty minutes.
So if he and Janice were to witness the 'fun',
and to keep their date with Dr Septic, it was
high time they were off!

Two minutes later Janice and the Professor,
accompanied by their bodyguards, were
thundering towards the doomed town in her
monstrous, bright yellow **iSPLATZ-U**™ 4x4 vehicle.

Behind it was a large trailer carrying a huge and ultra-luxurious motor yacht, of the sort owned by royalty and billionaires.

Johnny Catbiscuit had also just completed a calculation. He'd worked out that he and Felix were going to die in the next two minutes. Because that's how long it would take for the fizzing flame to reach the bonfire.

'After which,' said Felix Pawson, **'WHOOOOSH!'**

'That's one thing I like about having you with me in a crisis, FP,' said Johnny. 'You're always so positive and reassuring!'

74

'It's my naturally sunny personality!' quipped Felix. 'But I do suppose it's about time we started thinking how we're going to get out of this little fix.'

'Me too!' said Johnny.

And they both began applying their huge brainpower to their predicament. However, after thirty seconds of intense concentration, and for the first time ever, they could think of nothing. They were stumped! It looked like their glorious, but tragically short, superhero careers were about to go up in flames!

But then, just as both of them were mutually lamenting all those adventures they would

75

never share, they heard a voice say, 'Hang on there, chaps, I'm coming as fast as I can!'

They scanned the yard. Neither of them were able to spot the voice's owner.

But here it was again! 'Sorry about the delay. My old legs aren't what they used to be!'

At which point Felix said, 'I spy with my little eye an extremely crusty, walking meat pie!'

Johnny assumed that the stressful nature of their predicament had caused Felix to flip. But then *he* spotted the meat pie! What appeared to be a golden-brown cornish pasty, or a large and overcooked samosa, was slowly making its way across the yard towards the fizzing fuse.

'Going as fast as I can,' said the samosa. 'Just hope I can make it in time!'

**'SHIVERING SHOWER-CURTAINS!'** yelled Felix. 'It's a blinking tortoise!'

'Less of the blinking!' said the cornish pasty. 'And the name's Peter.'

'Well, hiyah, Peter!' cried Felix. 'Are we glad to see you!'

'How come you didn't get locked in the feed store?' asked Johnny.

'Pretended to be a rock,' said Peter, who was now only a few centimetres from the flame.

'Go on, go for it, old fellah!' Johnny and Felix yelled in unison, their hearts in their

mouths. 'A final sprint and you can do it!'

'What's a "sprint"?' said Peter.

But then he did something remarkable, which the intrepid twosome coudn't believe! Peter paused, stood on tiptoe, took a deep breath, drew his head into his shell, then did a stupendous four-footed take-off, launching himself at least three whole centimetres through the air, and landing slap-bang on top of the flame, which went out in an instant!

Then, head out again, he said, 'Now are you satisfied?'

'Brilliant!' said Felix. 'OK! What are you like at chewing?'

'Hmmm!' said Peter. 'Not so hot. I've only got two teeth. And they're blunt.'

'But ours aren't!' cried other voices.

Johnny and Felix turned to see two squirrels scampering towards them.

'Sorry we didn't get here sooner!' one of the squirrels said breathlessly. 'We've only just heard you were in trouble, Johnny Catbiscuit. The house martins who nest in the old barn

told us. Reinforcements are on the way!'

A minute later, hundreds and hundreds of mice, rats, shrews, voles, dormice, squirrels and other wild creatures came swarming out of the woods and fields surrounding Safe Pastures. Soon there were so many of them clambering over the super-duo that Johnny and Felix disappeared from sight. They all set

about furiously **NIBBLING**, *CHEWING* and **gnawing** through that great swathe of netting, while others ran to help the staff in the feed store.

'It's about time you lot got round to saving *us*!' joked Johnny.

'The pleasure's all ours!' said a dormouse, through a mouthful of **THEWLON**™. 'I can't think of anyone more deserving!'

And the plucky pair's rescue by this regiment of rodents didn't come a moment too soon! For now that great wall of water and its cargo of tentacled monsters had left the dam far behind and was hurtling relentlessly towards the first of its ill-fated victims!

## CHAPTER EIGHT
## DISASTER!

The children on the bus going towards the iron bridge which straddled the sheer walls of Torrent-Head Gorge had no idea what lay in store. Their aeroplane had landed thirty minutes earlier and they were on their way home to Nothingham-on-Torrent, looking forward to telling everyone about their brilliant holiday!

But what they were really excited about was seeing the handsome young superhero Johnny

82

Catbiscuit and his cool-cat sidekick Felix Pawson rocketing past them. They were still finding it extremely hard to believe that they'd actually seen them!

They were also being entertained, if slightly terrified, by the mad-looking, sooty-faced woman with the zigzag hairstyle in a huge, yellow iSPLATZ-U™ vehicle. She'd been trying to overtake their bus at every hairpin bend in the road for the last three miles. A very dangerous thing to do! Especially when you're towing a trailer with an enormous yacht!

The mad woman finally roared past them, shaking her fist, then slapping the bald and

83

shiny head of the small, fat man sitting next to her. A moment later, the **iSPLATZ-U**™ and the giant boat were a distant speck.

Only half a kilometre to the north of those children, the stupendous surge of water and its beastly burden of squirming flesh was roaring down the upper Torrent valley with stupefying speed. It was a relentless rush of chaos and destruction. Trees, boulders, stone walls, barns and farm vehicles were all caught up in its sinister, swirling swell. Tractors bobbed and whirled, tossed about like toys. Enormous trees which had stood firm for centuries were wrenched from the earth, then thrown about

the foaming Torrent as if they were twigs.

Sheep, horses and cattle stampeded up steep hillsides to escape the terrible tide. Small animals scrambled up trees, clinging desperately to branches when they crashed into the water, and hanging on for dear life as they hurtled along with the flood.

85

But so far, because of the isolated nature of the upper Torrent Valley, and the swift evasive action of the animals, not a single human or creature had perished.

All that was about to change.

The road to Torrent-Head Gorge passed through a steep-sided cutting, so it was impossible for the children's bus driver to see, or even hear, the great rushing wall of water which was now only metres from the bridge. It was only as he emerged that he realised anything was amiss. But by then it was too late. Because his bus was on the bridge.

The water hit the bridge with all the force of

a juggernaut being driven into a doll's house. As it did so, there was a great grinding and shuddering noise and the huge metal columns **snapped** like knitting needles, taking the road with them and leaving nothing in front of the bus but thin air! An instant later it, too, was **PLUMMETING** into the gorge.

Johnny and Felix arrived just in time to see the bus driving on to the bridge and the fearsome flood about to hit. After that, everything seemed to happen in slow motion. The great bridge toppled into the water, the bus leapt out into nothingness, and the monstrous creatures **THRASHED** and **WRITHED** in the waters

87

below. All this was accompanied by the screams of the terrified children.

The only thing which didn't appear to be moving in slow motion was Johnny Catbiscuit. Like a hawk dropping on its prey, he **HURTLED** towards the **PLUMMETING** bus with such speed and purpose that he appeared as a shimmering blur of movement and light.

A picosecond later, he seized the bus's roof rack, gripping it with all his might. Then, using the momentum of his downward swoop, and an **ALMIGHTY SURGE** of super-power, he swept skywards, the bus dangling beneath him.

For the children on that bus it was an

experience without equal. An experience that they would tell to their own children. And their children's children. Over and over again!

But right then, it was all absolutely terrifying! One moment they'd been chatting happily, and the next they'd been **PLUMMETING** towards the churning flood and those swirling, seething tentacled terrors. Fortunately, they were all wearing seatbelts.

All apart from one little boy who, despite being told again and again to fasten his, still wasn't wearing it. The consequences of which were terrible!

## CHAPTER NINE
# CRUNCH!

As Johnny seized the roof rack, halting the bus's fall in an instant, and saving the lives of all those children, the unlucky little lad was catapulted straight through its open sunroof and into the foaming frenzy below. Where he wouldn't have survived a minute, had it not been for Felix Pawson.

Seeing the boy fall from the bus, Felix leapt from Johnny's back without a moment's

91

thought for his own safety, landing in the swirling water just a few metres away from the spluttering, choking child. He yelled, 'Surely you weren't that desperate for a bath!'

Then he began to **WHIZZ** through the water, his arms and legs a haze of movement! Just in time. Because one massive and revolting bulbous-brained example of Professor Troll's handiwork had spotted the boy, too. Writhing and twisting through the foaming flood, it began to ooze its way towards him. The gasping boy, normally a strong swimmer, was wide-eyed with terror, paralysed by the sight of the billowing beast. In the next instant, its massive

tentacles encircled his waist, then began squeezing the life out of him, as it dragged him below the seething surface of the Torrent, and prepared to tear him limb from limb.

A huge charge of super-adrenaline filled Felix. He **SHOT** out of the flood, leaping on to the creature's tentacles and furiously sinking his razor-sharp teeth into them over and over again. Then he fastened himself to the monster's

great pulpy head and sank his claws and fangs into its brain and its eyes! His bites and scratches were so ferocious that the great monster slackened its hold on the boy. He wriggled free and thrust himself back into fresh air. A moment later, his shirt hooked on a tree branch. He was safe.

But Felix Pawson wasn't! The breath was being squeezed out of him by the terrifying tentacles of yet another of those squelchy horrors! It pulled him under the water, dragging him towards a huge warty growth, where cupid-like lips opened to reveal a cavernous mouth. As the water filled his lungs and the lips fastened

around him, Felix wondered which would be worse, to die by drowning, or by being eaten alive? He didn't get the chance to decide, because suddenly there was a torpedo shooting towards him. But it wasn't a torpedo. It was **JOHNNY CATBISCUIT!**

An instant later, head down, arms pressed to his sides, Johnny powered into the monster with such force that it **EXPLODED** out of the water, leaping six metres into the air! Johnny followed, bursting from the surface like a missile launched from a submarine. Then, seizing the creature by its tentacles, he whirled it around his head so violently that it released

Felix, who dropped safely to the grass below.

Johnny **HURTLED** towards the jagged, broken metal columns of the bridge, the creature dangling beneath him. Then, hovering above the sharpest and most jagged of them all, he dropped it. There was a horrible '**SQUISH!**', and a noise like the air being let out of a tyre, as the spike penetrated the creature's body.

Felix yelled, '*ANYONE FANCY A FISH KEBAB?*'

For a moment or two the creature thrashed about, trying to free itself from the stake. Then it went still.

The children from the bus, who stood at the gorge's edge watching this great drama unfold,

97

gave a huge cheer. But the super-duo didn't hear it. For they were already rocketing away, desperate to reach Nothingham-on-Torrent before the great wave of terror did!

And for those very tired children, this astounding day of drama and spectacle *still* wasn't over! Now they heard the roar of engines. A convoy of vehicles was approaching the Torrent-Head Gorge at phenomenal speed! And because their vision was obscured by the high embankments and the road's twists and turns, the drivers were completely unaware of the horrible fate which awaited them!

98

As he followed his speeding convoy, Dr Septic was feeling very pleased with himself. Because everything was going splendidly! And, as he often did when he was alone, he was talking to himself. **'OH JOY OF JOYS!'** he shrieked, furiously spinning the steering wheel of his shining limousine as it screeched around bend after bend. 'I've finally rid myself of the accursed Catbiscuit. And his pesky pussy cat sidekick!'

Then he roared with insane laughter and punched the air victoriously, stamping so hard on the accelerator of his limo that it rocketed towards the next bend. **YESSS!** He was free to

pursue his plan to overwhelm the Realms, without interference from that most resourceful, resilient and resolute of superheroes!

In twenty minutes, he and his army of thugs would triumphantly enter Nothingham-on-Torrent. Then his brutes would have some sport in their motor dinghies, attacking the few wretches who'd survived the great flood and its tentacled terrors with their harpoons.

And Dr Septic would oversee their cruel campaign of carnage from the bridge of his yacht, the lovely Janice at his side, and himself in his new captain's cap and sailor suit. After which they would move on to the next flooded

town and repeat the process, until the whole of the Realms was conquered.

But what was this? Dr Septic's 'delightful' daydream was suddenly interrupted by the sound of screeching brakes, followed by the smell of burning rubber. And now, as he rounded a corner, he saw something which made his **BLOOD FREEZE** and his **STOMACH CHURN!** As he looked on in utter, disbelieving horror, the first five vehicles of his convoy leapt off the gorge's edge, then **PLUNGED** into the great void where the bridge had stood just minutes

earlier. The vehicles following screeched to a stop, not going over the edge as the others had done, but simply 'concertinaing' into each other – **CRUNCH! CRUNCH! CRUNCH! CRUNCH!** – then teetering on the brink of the gorge.

And there they would have stayed, if their glorious leader hadn't gone hurtling into them with a huge **SMASH!** He still had his accelerator foot pressed hard to the floor because he was only half with-it, having been so abruptly awoken from his daydream. So, before his thugs could abandon their trucks, Dr Septic shunted what remained of his murderous

army over the cliff. The same cliff over which he also plunged an instant later.

As his shimmering, silver, open-topped car **PLUMMETED** towards the Torrent, Dr Septic gazed down at the smashed vehicles and the broken bodies of his troops. Some of them littered its rocky banks, while others were being torn to pieces by the stragglers from Professor Troll's sinister shoal. He reflected that even the best-laid plans can go awry. And, just as he began to curse himself for not having foreseen all of the consequences of sending that massive wall of water racing down the Torrent Valley, everything went very, very dark.

## CHAPTER TEN

# NOTHINGHAM-UNDER-TORRENT

Had Johnny and Felix known of the terrible fate of Dr Septic's hench-thugs, they might have breathed a sigh of relief. But it would only have been a very brief one. Because now, having seen the true nature and fury of Professor Troll's awful creations, they were only too well aware of the terrible consequences for all the towns that lay in the path of Dr Septic's fearful flood. They were also only too well

aware that it was beyond even *their* boundless energies to save the countless people and animals it threatened. So, as they sped towards Nothingham, Johnny made a call to Jatinder, urging her to direct the superheroes to the communities further down the valley, where he knew that they would do their stuff!

It was a message which saved thousands. Aided by the emergency services, superheroes like CAPTAIN UNSTOPPABLE, DANGER DUDE, SUSAN the Human-Post-It-Note and the FLYING FURY, among many others, swiftly and successfully evacuated the area. Not a single soul, animal or human, was in any way harmed.

105

But not so for Nothingham-on-Torrent! As Johnny was about to hang up, Jatinder received the news that none of them wanted to hear. The great wall of water and its cargo of calamity had just swept into that unlucky town.

Johnny and Felix exchanged grim looks. Getting everyone out safely would now be a hundred times more difficult, if not impossible.

'Looks like Dr Septic might have got the better of us after all,' Felix said.

'No he hasn't! I've got an idea!' Johnny replied.

A nano-second later, he halted his headlong flight, left Felix to make his own way to the flooded town, and **ROCKETED** off to the east!

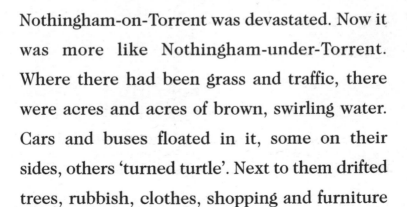

Nothingham-on-Torrent was devastated. Now it was more like Nothingham-under-Torrent. Where there had been grass and traffic, there were acres and acres of brown, swirling water. Cars and buses floated in it, some on their sides, others 'turned turtle'. Next to them drifted trees, rubbish, clothes, shopping and furniture

and, occasionally, a small creature which hadn't escaped the flood's deathly grasp.

Dr Septic's great wave of terror was rushing onwards towards the other towns and villages of the Torrent Valley. But those dark and sinister waters continued to flow into Nothingham, lapping menacingly at the roofs and treetops from which terrified faces, both human and animal, gazed out at this great flood. They knew it would soon overwhelm them.

To add to the misery of those unlucky townsfolk and their pets, an enormous and luxurious motor yacht was cruising the streets of their drowned town. And it was obvious that

the boat and its freakish crew weren't here to rescue the stranded families and their animals.

Quite alarmingly, it appeared that they were here for 'fun'! For every time that monstrous supercruiser passed a rooftop where a family perched precariously with their precious pets, or a tree where half-drowned cats, guinea pigs, hamsters and other pitiful creatures clung desperately to its uppermost branches, Janice Evil, reclining on the yacht's sun-deck, would scream, 'Now, Boris! Get them now!'

Obeying orders, the black-uniformed brute at the boat's controls would gun its engines, cutting through the water as close as he could

to the terrified victims. And then, as the yacht's huge bow-wave SURGED over shivering children, howling animals and terrified adults, all but drowning them, the horrible woman would shriek with mirth and squeal, 'Oh, that was fun! Do it again, Boris!'

Then the brute would do it again, terrifying his

victims out of their wits and causing the woman to shriek even more gleefully and hysterically. She would then turn to the tubby little man in the pink shorts and crimson bowtie and squeal, 'Little robot! Little, little robot! Don't you just love messing about in boats!'

This was pushing Professor Troll's already dangerously high blood pressure to boiling point! Mad Janice's fun and games were the last thing he needed. He was already beside himself with worry about Dr Septic. He should have come sailing into Nothingham-on-Torrent at least half an hour ago. But that didn't worry Janice one jot! She was having too much fun!

111

For the stranded families and their pets, even *this* wasn't the worst of their predicament. What really terrified them more than anything, on this, the most horror-filled day of their lives, were the hideous, many-tentacled monsters which squirmed and seethed in the ever-rising waters. For they were creatures the likes of which the families had never seen before. Hundreds and hundreds of great billowing, bulbous-eyed things, bristling with snaking tentacles, living warts and vicious beaks. And

they weren't going any-
where. For all around
them was the flesh they
craved, both human and

animal. And they were all very, very hungry.
And already stalking their prey!

Every now and again, a huge pulpy head
would emerge from the gloop and a pair of evil,
bulging eyes would hungrily survey the people

and animals clinging to
their fast-shrinking islands
of hope. Then its tentacles
would snake up towards a
rooftop and attempt to

wrap themselves around a pet or child, narrowly missing them as they scrambled even higher.

And now, the inevitable happened. As marooned families looked on in horror, one particularly large and many-tentacled monstrosity pressed itself against the side of a submerged house, reaching for a pathetically howling pet Labrador. The dog had slipped from the ridge above and was slowly sliding towards the water, scrabbling frantically at the tiles in a vain attempt to save itself. A boy and a girl screamed, **'NO! NO! NOT OUR LOVELY BARNY!'** and also slid down the roof, in a brave attempt to rescue it. And, as the great monster's tentacles

encircled the dog, the children seized it too!

Now began a furious tug of war, with the children grimly clinging to their pet, as the monster wrapped more of its frantically waving, finger-like tentacles around the dog's trembling body. But the young ones' strength was no match for the huge beast. A moment later it pulled both dog and children into the water.

Alerted by this great commotion, more of the pulpy monsters began to **OOZE** and **WRIGGLE** towards this life-or-death struggle. Soon, those ravenous creatures had enfolded the screaming kids and doomed dog in their fearsome feelers and the inevitable gory outcome of this terrible conflict became plain for all to see. Within seconds, this heroic drama would be transformed into a stomach-churning feeding frenzy!

But then came a cry of, 'Look! Over there!' and someone pointed to the powerful figure which was now leaping from rooftop to rooftop towards this thrashing, squirming knot of terror. The powerful figure of Felix Pawson.

## CHAPTER ELEVEN
# JOHNNY TO THE RESCUE!

Springing from the final rooftop as if shot from a cannon, and with a cry of, '**PICK ON SOMEONE YOUR OWN SIZE! YOU BUG-EYED BLOBS OF BLANCMANGE!**', Felix hurled himself into the writhing mass of monsters. He changed into a *SPITTING*, *HISSING* fireball of fury and tore into them with tooth and claw, ripping great strips of flesh from their jelly-like bodies and sinking his

117

fangs into them over and over again.

It was an awesome thing to see. So awesome that, inspired by the bravery of the silver-clad super-cat, ordinary men and women began yelling, 'Come on, everyone! Don't leave him to do it all on his own! We can help, too!' and heroically hurling themselves into the water and swimming towards the great struggle.

But this was a foolhardy, if courageous, thing to do. Because these mere mortals were no match for the terrifying tentacled monsters. Now dozens of potential victims were within their reach, hundreds of them turned towards the swimmers. Soon, almost all of Professor

Troll's hideous creations had the humans encircled and were moving in for the kill.

And still Felix Pawson continued his valiant battle, fighting so ferociously that the children and dog remained unharmed. But soon even *his* energies began to dwindle and he knew that he could not hold off the monsters much longer. Despite the heroism of both cat and humans, it looked like a gory massacre was about to take place.

But then, just as Felix Pawson was sent spinning by a devastating blow from a lashing tentacle, a great shout of, **'HANG ON IN THERE, FP!'** rang out, and the watchers on

119

the rooftops and in the trees turned to see an amazing sight.

Hundreds of leaping dolphins raced into the flooded town. Behind them followed whales, basking sharks and sea lions. And sitting astride the largest dolphin, urging them all on like a general leading his army into battle, was Johnny Catbiscuit!

Johnny back-flipped into the flood and disappeared below the surface. The dolphins sped towards the endangered humans, intent on putting themselves between the people and the monsters. Then, as everyone swam for their lives, the dolphins launched their assault, ramming and butting, and taking great bites out of the monsters with their sharp, conical teeth. The tentacled fiends were no match for them. Not even their COILING, WRITHING, SNAPPING, TEARING feelers! For every time those terrible tentacles lashed out at them, the dolphins would leap right out of the flood, twisting and turning as they did,

leaving them grasping at nothing. Then the dolphins would re-launch their attack, devastating Professor Troll's hungry horrors with a ferocity and efficiency that was breathtaking to behold!

As the whales, whale sharks, basking sharks and sea lions joined the dolphins in this marine battle to end all marine battles, Felix Pawson was at last able to get the children and their half-drowned dog back on to the rooftop. Six huge basking sharks had come to his rescue, turning the tentacled monsters into a bloody mess of severed tentacles and ripped flesh in no time, and causing Felix to yell, 'Bet that came as a bite of a shark!'

And while Felix was doing something which surprised even him, giving the 'kiss-of-life' to a half-drowned dog, the dolphins began to herd the remaining sea monsters into a flooded car park. It was surrounded on all sides by tall buildings, making escape impossible. But as they did so, there was a thunderous roar, and the yacht, this time with the mad woman at its wheel, raced towards the dolphins.

'Watch this, you wimps!' she screamed. 'I'll slice them all into sardines with our propeller blades. They won't stand a chance. And you two!' she yelled at the two thugs. 'Pick off the survivors with your harpoon guns!'

123

It certainly did look like Janice and her brutes would succeed in killing the brave dolphins and other sea creatures. But then, as the good folk of Nothingham-on-Torrent looked on in utter amazement, something quite astonishing happened. All at once, the boat stopped! Dead in the water, as if it had been seized by a giant invisible hand. The two thugs were hurled into the midst of the trapped sea monsters. The results of this were so unpleasant that the watching grown-ups not only covered their children's eyes, but their own eyes, too!

'FLYING FLIP-FLOPS!' screamed Janice, revving the boat's engines with all her might

and still going nowhere. 'What is going on? Some bilge-bucket must have put the blinking brakes on!'

Which was far from the truth, not to mention a silly thing to say! Because, several metres beneath her, Johnny Catbiscuit was making use of his astounding ability to remain under water for hours on end without having to come up for air, or without his skin going pruney! Using his super-strength, he was gripping the boat's hull and grinning as he thought how much this must be frustrating Janice.

And he was right. She was now revving the engine so fiercely that, fearing for his life,

125

Professor Troll rushed at her and tried to take over the controls, yelling, '**STOP IT, YOU BATTY OLD BACON-BURGER**, you'll blow us sky-high!'

The furious Janice turned to Professor Troll and said, 'What did you just call me?'

'I called you a batty old bacon-burger, you hideous old harpy!' shouted Professor Troll. And then he ran away, with Janice in hot pursuit! Round and round the boat they went, with Janice screaming, 'Just wait 'till I catch you, little robot! I'll trash your transformer, crush your condensers and stamp on your spark plugs until your oscillators drop off!'

Then, with a cry of, '*OH, WHAT THE HELICOPTERS!*'

Professor Troll turned on his pursuer, put down his head, and charged her like a bull, head-butting her with such force that he flipped her straight over the side of the boat.

Now things began to happen at a furious pace. For, as bonkers Janice thrashed about in the water screaming, **'HELP ME! HELP ME!**

SOMEONE HELP ME, PLEASE! MY EYE MAKE-UP IS RUNNING! AND I CAN'T SWIM!', there was an answering cry of, 'Do not fear, my dear! Your beloved Septikins is here!' and a motor dinghy came hurtling around a corner with Dr Septic at the helm in his ripped and filthy sailor suit and crumpled captain's hat.

He had Janice on board his boat in a flash! Then, putting his false hand around her waist, he bent her over backwards and said, in a voice which sounded like broken glass being chewed by a Tyrannosaurus, 'Did you think I would forsake you, MY IKKLE WIKKLE FLUFFY BUNNY?' and gave her a huge wet kiss. Then he seized

the dinghy's rudder and roared off, with the sobbing Janice draped around his neck.

For, unlike his hench-thugs, Dr Septic had survived his fall. When he had plunged into the flood, he had been thrown clear of his open-topped limousine and landed comfortably, and very conveniently, in one of the inflatable dinghies which had been strapped to the roof racks of the other vehicles. And then, having the 'luck of the diabolical', as he liked to put it, once he'd recovered, he had zoomed off in the boat for Nothingham.

As Dr Septic and Janice fled the scene of their crimes, Johnny *SHOT* out of the water

129

like a projectile from its launcher. The dolphins were out of danger and Dr Septic was escaping! That dinghy was no match for Johnny's powers! He would catch him in an instant!

But then he heard a scream and turned to see Professor Troll being held aloft in the tentacle of the biggest and most ferocious and, for that matter, single surviving specimen of his creations. It had broken through the cordon of dolphins and snatched the Professor from the deck of the yacht.

Johnny Catbiscuit was faced with a most terrible dilemma. Should he pursue Dr Septic? Or save Professor Troll?

## CHAPTER TWELVE
# BURP!

Johnny Catbiscuit was a superhero and superheroes are pledged to save lives, wherever and whenever they can. And Johnny wasn't about to break his pledge. So, putting away thoughts of Dr Septic, he turned away from his fleeing foe and went to the Professor's rescue.

But he got a shock. The Professor wasn't there any more. In the split second when Johnny had been torn between pursuit and rescue,

the Professor's creation had popped him into its mouth and swallowed him in one gulp.

As Felix Pawson later said, it was a case of, **'PREPARE TO EAT THY MAKER!'**

And now, watched by hundreds, Professor Troll was making the long and uncomfortable journey through the creature's see-through digestive system. It wasn't a pretty sight!

Johnny knew that once the Professor reached its stomach, its digestive juices would go to work on him and he would soon become a sort of scholarly **MUSH**. So Johnny got ready to get him out of there. A task he didn't relish! But then something unexpected happened.

The monster let out an enormous **BURP!** Then another! And then it *regurgitated* Professor Troll on to the deck of the yacht, in a spectacularly soupy and sickening shower of saliva and digestive juices.

'Gross!' said Johnny.

Looking the worse for wear, but still alive, Professor Troll seized his chance, grabbed the boat's controls and was off like a shot, leaving Johnny open-mouthed with amazement.

Johnny clambered on to a rooftop, and joined Felix. They stared at the very poorly-looking sea monster. For, despite having **PUKED** up a Professor, it still didn't look at all well.

Felix nudged his super-partner and quipped, 'Ah, so this is the sick squid you owed me!'

At this point the chums spotted the real cause of the monster's discomfort. Lodged in its intestine was an enormous peanut butter sandwich which must have fallen from the Professor's pocket. And it appeared that the creature had a fatal peanut butter allergy because three seconds later, it died.

Now, helped by the dolphins and other sea creatures, Johnny and Felix set about ferrying the stranded humans and animals of Nothingham to places of safety. As they worked, Felix complimented Johnny on his

spectacular and impressive entrance into the drowned town, saying, 'It was no fluke, you coming to the rescue like that.'

'Too right!' Johnny replied, 'I definitely did it on porpoise!'

Three hours later, the flood began to recede from the drowned town. Helped by emergency workers from as far afield as Busyville, Shiverpool and Londonland, the super-duo began the task of checking flooded buildings. And their energies weren't wasted. For as they went from house to house, they came across many little creatures which had been left

behind in the great rush to escape the tide of terror. And a few humans, too! But in almost every case they were unharmed, and were reunited with their loved ones.

As Johnny and Felix were saving those grateful survivors from their water-logged hidey-holes, unknown to them they were being observed. Back at Septic Towers, Dr Septic was studying the super-duo's every move through the lens of his spectographic telescope, grinding his teeth in frustration and furiously tearing his ruined sailor suit with his false hand.

But the evil maniac had a couple of consolations. For even now, the cogs of his

brilliant mind were working flat-out on his next sinister scheme to bring misery and mayhem to the Realms and the superheroes. Particularly to Johnny Catbiscuit and Felix Pawson!

And then there were the deeply satisfying HOWLS of anguish he could hear coming from a rat-infested dungeon, deep below Septic Towers. A rat-infested dungeon where Janice Evil had chained Professor Troll to a slimy and putrid wall, two metres away from which, and only just out of his reach, was a table groaning with dozens of peanut butter sandwiches.

Professor Troll wasn't the only one who was ravenous. With their work over and back in

138

their day-to-day incarnations, Wayne Bunn and Felix Pawson arrived back at Wayne's gran's. She'd gone to bed, exhausted by a day of watching TV news about floods and fearsome multi-tentacled octopus monsters. But, caring as ever, she had left a note telling her beloved grandson that his tea was by the microwave.

'What is it?' said Felix, as Wayne uncovered the plate.

'Fish fingers!' said Wayne.

# THE END

# Professor Elvis Troll

## FULL NAME

Professor Elvis Ricky Dwayne Pernicious Herman T. Troll Jr PHD; DIPI (1st class); ABC; 123; I. Bizi B.

## FAMILY BACKGROUND

Small, bald and tubby. Wears cravats or bow ties with crackly nylon shirts and baggy shorts, or tight, checked trousers.

## FIRST MEETING WITH DR SEPTIC

In HMP 'The Naughty Corner': high-security correction centre for badly-behaved five-year-olds. Elvis (nicknamed Jelly-Belly) was in for

stealing a jar of peanut butter jelly. Dr Septic (Stick Insect) for many, many crimes.

## MAIN OCCUPATION

Creating horrid monstrosities to bring terror and misery to the Realms of Normality. For example, Piranha Face Ferguson, a seven-foot-tall, bullet-proof, cart-wheeling cannibal, human from the neck down and snapping piranha from the neck up; Hairy Mary the Really Scary Little Fairy, pretty, but a massively bearded, fire-breathing seven-year-old who can be 'a handful', in the words of Inspector Hector Vector; and Boris and Betty Bullwinkle, terrifying gigantic twin

babies who are delivered to their target town in a huge lorry advertising **FREE MONEY - HERE TODAY!** guaranteeing them a supply of victims (see *Johnny Catbiscuit and the Stolen Secrets*).

## FIRST PROJECT WITH DR SEPTIC

'Jelly-Belly' and 'Stick Insect' dug a tunnel with dessert spoons and plastic sand-tray shovels, then told the other kids it was a chocolate mine. They tipped off the warders to a mass breakout. They escaped by shooting themselves from a rocket launcher made of plastic construction bricks, elastic bands, big dustbins and lard.

'JB' and 'SI' lived in the woods and

survived on dew, dandelion leaves and raw
squirrels for ten years. They read stolen
library books and discussed plans for 'World
Domination'. They were finally recaptured.
Both had the DIY equivalent of university
degrees in twenty-three subjects, including
advanced genetics, zoology, bio-engineering,
brick-laying, leisure centre management and
home brain surgery.

## OUT AGAIN

'JB' and 'SI' were released three days after
recapture due to a legal mix-up. They split
after a tiff over a lost library card. Elvis
became Professor of Everything and set up a

'Bonsai Ant' business. But his stock 'disappeared' and he fled the country, living rough on the streets of Shockholm, Snowberia.

Dr Septic – now the third richest man on Space-Speck Earth – was in Shockholm for the top secret '**MOST EVIL PEOPLE**' annual get-together. He found Elvis in an alley, sharing a jar of peanut butter with three huskies. They had a tearful reunion. Dr Septic offered him the job of scary fiends research and development manager. Elvis accepted.

## HOBBIES

Knitting his own underwear; stamp collecting; having nightmares; peanut butter.

# Janice Evil

## FAMILY BACKGROUND

Tall, with orange skin, a pouting bottom lip you could stand a TV on, sticky-out eyes that appear to look everywhere at once, 'sap-blonde' hair i.e. with a greenish hue, as if it's infested with mildew (which it is) and really scary 'predator' teeth. Janice is a keen fan of cosmetic surgery and, with the exception of her brain and eyes, her entire body has been

replaced several times over; she is already on her third nose and fourth set of lips.

She wears only unique and 'exclusive' fashion items. Her entire wardrobe consists of outfits created from endangered species. Her favourite is a mini-skirt made from the last blue-nosed leopard on Space-Speck Earth.

## PERSONALITY TRAITS

Notorious for her temper tantrums, during which she has been known to a) bite through a table leg b) punch six of Dr Septic's uber-thugs unconscious c) spit real venom and d) throw Professor Troll from the topmost tower of Dr Septic's mountain fortress.

# Janice Evil

## EVIL HABITS

a) Making 'hit lists' of people who have offended her e.g. people who are more beautiful than she is, then getting Dr Septic to do horrid things to them; b) taking potshots at songbirds and woodland creatures with her hyper-powerful laser-guided catapult; c) wandering around with a pair of garden shears, looking for slugs, ants and worms to cut in half.

## EARLY YEARS

Originally a trainee beautician but was dismissed for giving a fashion model the complexion of a one-hundred-year-old tortoise by covering her in quick-setting cement.

147

## OTHER CAREERS

Traffic warden, sewage engineer, clairvoyant, oil rig worker, trapeze artist, shepherdess, camel-jockey and lion tamer.

## FIRST MEETING WITH DR SEPTIC

Dr S. went to her salon for a manicure (half-price for him). A man cleaning the windows fell off his ladder and was trampled by a flock of sheep. Dr S. and Janice rolled around with laughter. Dr S. fell in love and asked her to be his nearest and cruellest. She said yes! They skipped off down the street (in slow motion), knocking over old people and stealing ice creams from children (also in slow motion).

## COMPLICATIONS AND INTRIGUES

Two days before meeting Dr S., J. married husband sixteen, billionaire cheese-maker, Horace Golightly. Consequences (as rumoured): a) Lured to remote picnic spot by J., H. was pounced on by Dr S.'s thugs, bundled into a really big jiffy bag and posted to an uninhabited location; or b) H. was kidnapped, taken to a dungeon in Septic Towers and 'persuaded' to sign over his vast fortune to Dr S. and J. Still there, with only rats and spiders for company.

## HOBBIES

Looking in mirrors, pouting, looking in mirrors, more pouting.

# SUPERHERO LANGUAGE

Knowing what to say in different superhero scenarios is very important, as it can have a big effect on the outcome of a rescue or confrontation situation. For instance, if you're rescuing a frail old lady from the eighteenth floor window ledge of a blazing skyscraper it isn't a good idea to yell,

## REACH FOR THE SKY, SCUMBUCKET!

as this could cause her to **A** have a heart attack; **B** leap off the ledge; or **C** climb back inside the burning building. It would be much better to say,

## DO NOT FEAR, EVERYTHING'S GOING TO BE JUST FINE! YOU'LL BE SAFE IN NO TIME!

So, here are some situations and an assortment of superhero expressions you might use them in. Match the correct one to the situation.

**1** RESCUING A YOUNG LADY FROM KIDNAPPERS, YOU FIND HER TIED TO A HYPER-SENSITIVE TRIP-WIRE, PRIMED TO BLOW UP THE ENTIRE PLANET IN JUST SIX SECONDS. WOULD YOU SAY . . .

**A** Oooh, I do like your shoes! Where did you get them from?

**B** I really will have this defused in a jiffy. As soon as I can get my hands to stop shaking!

**C** Slow and easy! You're far too beautiful to die. Ah, done it!

**D** You know, I can never remember. Is the live wire the red one? Or is it the green?

151

**2** A SMALL CHILD IS SEIZED BY HUNGRY GRIZZLY BEARS. THE FRANTIC PARENTS DON'T KNOW WHAT TO DO. ARRIVING AT THE CRISIS, WOULD YOU SAY . . .

**A** I really would like to help you. But you see, I've got this terrible allergy to fur.

**B** *TAKE THAT*, you walking hearthrugs! And that! **BLAM! SPLATT! ZAPP!** That's it, run for your lives, you pair of lily-livered old fleabags*!

**C** Don't worry! I've had to deal with a situation like this a couple of times before. And you never know, this one could be third time lucky!

**D** Sorry, no can do! Don't you realise that these animals are on the WWF Endangered Species list?!

**\*** NB: You say this to the bears, not the distraught parents.

152

**3** A COUPLE OF TEN-YEAR-OLDS ARE BLOWN OUT TO SEA IN A DINGHY AND THE WAVES ARE AS HIGH AS HOUSES. ON REACHING THEM, WOULD YOU SAY . . .

 **A** Oh dear, dear, dear! Aren't you a silly pair? Fancy going out in weather like this. I've a good mind to let you drown. Just to teach you both a lesson!

**B** I'm happy to save you. But it's going to cost you! How does £5,000 each sound? £2,000 now, and the rest next Tuesday.

 **C** Hmm, this is a tricky one. Not sure how to tackle it. But I know someone who will. Hang on. Be back in a couple of days.

 **D** Tough luck, guys! But you're safe now! Here, get stuck into this! I just happen to have this loaf of freshly-baked bread and flask of home-made, piping-hot beef broth in my backpack.

153

# EGMONT PRESS: ETHICAL PUBLISHING

Egmont Press is about turning writers into successful authors and children into passionate readers – producing books that enrich and entertain. As a responsible children's publisher, we go even further, considering the world in which our consumers are growing up.

**Safety First**
Naturally, all of our books meet legal safety requirements. But we go further than this; every book with play value is tested to the highest standards – if it fails, it's back to the drawing-board.

**Made Fairly**
We are working to ensure that the workers involved in our supply chain – the people that make our books – are treated with fairness and respect.

**Responsible Forestry**
We are committed to ensuring all our papers come from environmentally and socially responsible forest sources.

*For more information, please visit our website at*
*www.egmont.co.uk/ethicalpublishing*

---